BEASTS OF
OLYMPUS
UNICORN EMERGENCY

Beasts of Olympus series

BEASTS
OF
OLYMPUS
UNICORN EMERGENCY

LUCY COATS

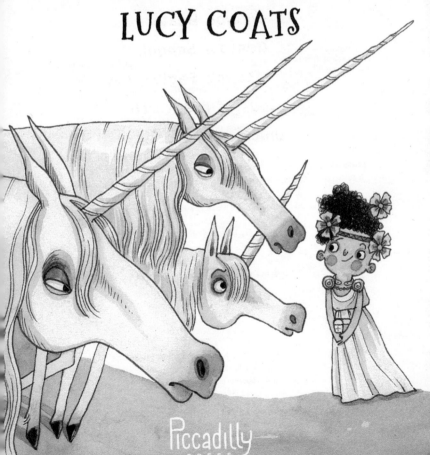

Piccadilly
PRESS

First published in Great Britain in 2018 by
Piccadilly Press
80-81 Wimpole Street, London, W1G 9RE
www.piccadillypress.co.uk

A CIP catalogue record for this book is available from the British Library.

ISBN: 978-1-848-12746-3

Typeset in opendyslexic
Printed and bound by Clays Ltd, Elcograf S.p.A.

Piccadilly Press is an imprint of Bonnier Zaffre,
a Bonnier Publishing Company
www.bonnierpublishingfiction.co.uk

For Linda and her grandchildren,
Jacob, Kyla and Carter

1

Farewell to Asgard

Demon cracked one eye open, groaning, and hurriedly shut it again. His brain felt as if Hephaestus the smith god had been hitting it with hammers, and there was a strange ringing sound in his ears. It had been a very late night.

"Go 'way!" he said, as a hand shook his shoulder roughly. "It's too early."

"No, it's not," said Thrud Thorsdaughter, his new friend, and the newest shield-maiden of Asgard. "You've been asleep ages. I haven't even been to bed yet," she added proudly.

Demon groaned again. The evening before was all a bit of a blur. There'd been a lot of very loud singing with Thrud's fellow maidens, and, once most of the gods had left, there had also been a great deal of toasting Demon's new status as holder of the Order of Yggdrasil.

The Valkyries had insisted he try a sip of their mead, which had made his head go all funny, and his knees wobble like a new-born lamb's. He seemed to remember some rather energetic dancing too. Sitting up cautiously, Demon opened his other eye.

"Tell me I didn't make a complete fool of myself last night," he said.

Thrud sniggered and hurriedly turned it into a cough.

"Let's just say that your version of the Bear Dance will go down in Asgard history, but your song about Fenrir needs some work on the wolf howling," she said. "Come on, you'll feel better after some breakfast."

The feasting hall of Valhalla was strewn with gnawed bones, overturned tables, empty mead flagons — and quite a few snoring bodies. The Asgardians definitely partied hard.

"I'm not really sure I feel much like breakfast," Demon said, avoiding a puddle of something questionable on the floor. "I think I'll go and check on Goldbristle instead."

Goldbristle was the boar who gave light to Asgard, who Demon had cured the day before, banishing the darkness caused by Loki, Thrud's evil uncle.

"Oh, he's long gone," said Thrud, skipping towards the doors and flinging them wide open, so that the diamond-bright light of day filled the hall. "Frey couldn't wait to drive up into the sky with him this morning. Doesn't it all look WONDERFUL?" she exclaimed.

Demon blinked and screwed up his eyes, trying hard to ignore the sensation of daggers being driven into his skull as a million rainbow reflections bounced off the snow-covered streets.

"Lovely," he muttered, putting his furry sheepskin hood up to block out

the rays. Just then, a huge golden-
haired god carrying a gigantic silver
hammer came striding into view.
It was Thor, god of thunder.

"Dad!" Thrud yelled, running out of
the door and leaping into his arms.

"How's my little shield-maiden?" Thor
asked, whirling her round. "Have you
tried out Mjölnirina yet?"

Thrud shook her head, stroking the
small silver hammer hanging at her belt.

"Not yet," she said. "I wanted to see
if she could beat your Mjölnir. Let's put
them through their paces." She turned
and beckoned to Demon. "Come on,
Olympus Boy. You can watch."

As she and Thor strode off down the snowy streets, Demon stumbled after them. His head now felt as if it was full of wet treacle. These Asgardians were very strange. How could Thrud and Thor talk about their hammers as if they were alive?

He soon found out. The minute they reached the other side of Asgard's high wall, Thrud and Thor began whirling Mjölnirina and Mjölnir round their heads.

"Whee!" yelled Thrud, letting go.

"Woohoo!" shouted Thor, launching Mjölnir upwards at exactly the same moment.

Demon's eyes nearly fell out of his head. Instead of rising and then falling

to the ground, the two hammers shot
up and up into the sky. When they were
no more than dark specks against the
blue, white clouds boiled up around
them. Thunder roared above, and then,
like two streaks of silver lightning, the
hammers returned to the ground, hitting
with an earth-shaking thump. Where
they landed, the snow began to steam
and hiss.

Thor held out his hand.

"Come, Mjölnir!" he roared, and the
huge hammer heaved itself out of the
earth and returned to his hand.

Demon blinked. It was as if the
hammer was alive and could understand.

"Come, Mjölnirina!" Thrud called.

Nothing happened.

"Mjölnirina, COME!" she called again. There was a sort of wet hiccup, and the little hammer slowly flipped and flopped its way to her over the snow, coming to rest at Thrud's feet.

"Hmmn," said Thor. "You may have to work on the obedience commands a bit. But good first effort." He grinned at Demon, showing very white teeth under a magnificent moustache. "Perhaps you have a potion for that, young Pandemonius?"

Demon grinned back, his headache finally lifting. It was hard to be formal with a god like Thor.

"Not me, Your Humungous

Hammeriness," he said. "My potions are strictly for sick beasts."

Thor clapped him on the shoulder, sending him flying into a nearby snow bank.

"By Odin's hat," the big god said, fetching Demon out with one meaty hand and dusting the ice him off clumsily. "I forgot my own strength again." Then he frowned.

"That reminds me. I went to check on Fenrir this morning. He's still asleep, but he does seem to be whimpering a lot."

Immediately, Demon felt guilty. The day before, he'd put the enormous wolf into a permanent sleep to stop him killing Odin, the king of the Asgardians. Fenrir's wolf mind was truly and properly lost to madness, but Demon still felt bad that he hadn't been able to cure him.

"Maybe he's having nightmares," said Thrud. "I don't suppose you can do much about those?"

"Nightmares are terrible things," said Thor. "I have them myself." He shuddered. "Dreamed I was being eaten by old Fafnir the ice dragon once, teeth crunching, flesh-tearing and all. Took me days to shake it off. Even Odin admitted that was a bad one when I told it to him."

"I might be able to do something," Demon said slowly, as they walked back into Asgard again. "But it would have to wait till I get back to Olympus. There's somebody there who is a specialist in dreams. His name is Morpheus."

"Would he come here?" Thrud asked.

"I think so," Demon said. "He helped me once before, when I had some mad horses to manage."

"Mad horses?" Thor asked. "That sounds like a good adventure. Tell us more."

So Demon told them about the mad man-eating mares that Horrible Heracles had left in his mum's village, and how Morpheus had given them permanent dreams of hay and peace.

"Sounds like just the god we need here," said Thor. "Fenrir will be dreaming of chasing fluffy bunnies in no time."

Just then, Demon saw a tall, curvy figure up ahead, wrapped in white furs. All around her the ice flowed into curving tendrils that exploded into bouquets of exquisite ice blossoms. It was Demeter, goddess of fruitfulness.

"Ah, there you are, Pandemonius," she said as she reached them. "My work here is done, now that Goldbristle is back in the sky. The apple trees are all back in fruit, and it's time we returned to Olympus. Gather your things and meet me at Heimdall's Gate. Hurry now."

Demon bowed.

"Yes, Your Fabulous Fruitiness,"
he said. "Right away." The Olympian
gods were much more formal than the
Asgardian ones, and he didn't want to
take the chance of being turned into a
giant peach, or something worse.

Once he'd gathered up his magic
medicine box, and stowed Far Caller,
the little horn Odin had given him,
Thrud led Demon to Heimdall's Gate,
where Demeter was already waiting.

"I'll miss you," said Thrud, giving him
a hug. "Come back soon!"

Demon hugged her back.

"Or you could come and visit
Olympus," he said, with an exaggerated
shiver. "We have proper sunshine there

— none of this freezy snow stuff!"

Thrud only laughed.

Demon looked around as he joined Demeter, expecting the cloud ship he'd arrived on to appear. But there was no ship, and nothing else visible. How were they going to return to Olympus?

Just then, Heimdall, the herald of Asgard, arrived. His white beard was plaited into three jutting forks, each with small icicles hanging from it. His eyes were the pale white-blue of an early winter sky.

"Ready?" he boomed.

Demeter nodded, gesturing Demon to stand beside her.

Heimdall took the golden horn that twisted round his body like a huge snake and blew it softly. This time, the sound Demon heard was like a crisp dip in a cold forest pool. All the hair on his body lifted, as a rainbow bridge spun forward out of nothing, filling the sky with colour.

"Step forward onto Bifrost, and state your destination," the god commanded.

Demeter walked confidently onto the rainbow, beckoning Demon to stand beside her with one imperious finger.

"Olympus!" she cried.

It was not at all like travelling on the Iris Express, who was an opinionated rainbow goddess. Bifrost was more like a moving road, and Demon wasn't sure whether it was a god or not, as so far it was silent. He tried not to look down at the earth, so far below, as they sped forwards. The icy wind whipped his hair around his cheeks, blowing his hood off, and Demon clutched his coat around him. Gradually, though, the air got warmer and warmer, and by the time they approached Olympus, he was becoming uncomfortably hot.

"Phew!" said Demeter, making a very ungoddess-like flapping gesture with her hand as she stepped off the rainbow road. At once, all her furs disappeared, leaving her in her usual white goddess robes, and she vanished with a sparkle of lights and a delicious smell of ripe orchards.

"Not a word of thanks, as usual," said a gruff voice. "Typical goddess."

"Um, thank you for getting me back home safely," Demon said, trying to shed his woolly coat and boots.

"My pleasure," said Bifrost, just as a familiar flurry of colours arched down out of the evening sky.

"And just who is THIS intruder?" purred Iris the rainbow goddess dangerously, twining herself around the bridge.

"Iris, meet Bifrost, Bifrost, meet Iris," said Demon, deciding to leave undressing till later. There had been a distinct edge to Iris's voice – one he knew all too well. "I'll, er . . . just leave you two to it, shall I?" he said, hurrying off in the direction of the Stables of the Gods.

Demon knew a goddess in a temper when he heard one, and it was always best to move far, far away for fear of being turned into something unnatural.

2

Star Nymphs, Ahoy!

The stables were quiet as Demon
approached, panting. The sooner he got
rid of the rest of his hot, furry Asgard
clothes and put on something normal,
the better.

"Hey, Pan's scrawny kid," said Arnie
the griffin, flying down off its perch
on the roof. "How was the frozen
North? Did you bring me back a nice big
reindeer leg to chew on?"

"Unfortunately not," said Demon.
"But I did have an adventure with some

dark elves and a very scary dragon. I'll tell you all about it once I've got out of all this hot stuff."

The griffin cocked its head sideways, looking at him out of one orange eye.

"Your face does look a bit like the red part of old Heffy's forge," Arnie said. "All glowing and shiny."

Demon rolled his eyes. "Thanks for the compliment," he said.

Quickly, he dumped his bag, along with the magic medicine box, and ran up the stairs to the loft above the stables where he slept. It was a big relief to strip off his Asgardian kit, put on his tunic and feel cool again. When he climbed down again, his assistant,

Bion the faun, was there, fending off the griffin, who was pecking at his small hooves.

"Leave Bion alone, Arnie," Demon said crossly. "You know he doesn't like you doing that."

By the time he had inspected the stables and told Bion and the griffin all about his adventures, Demon was yawning. His late night with the Valkyries was definitely catching up with him.

"I'm going to turn in," he said. "I'll leave you to do the last checks, Bion."

"Sweet dreams," said Arnie, flapping off to its perch for the night.

Demon stopped dead. How could he have forgotten? He'd promised to send Morpheus to Asgard. But how was he to get hold of the god of dreams?

Suddenly he remembered. Morpheus had given him a shiny black crystal dreamcatcher, and asked him to wear it all year as payment for giving the mad mares good dreams. It was supposed to capture and hold all Demon's dreams, though he wasn't sure what the god wanted them for. Maybe he could contact Morpheus through that.

Fumbling right at the bottom of his pouch, his fingers touched something curiously squidgy. He pulled out a shiny, black crystal, whose edges seemed to blur and shift. Clutching it in his hand, Demon climbed up to the loft and fell into bed, snuggling down under his familiar spidersilk blanket as he stared into the dreamcatcher's depths. The rainbows swirling within it were . . . so . . . soothing . . .

"Please, Morpheus, help Fenrir," Demon whispered as his eyelids drooped shut.

Almost immediately, or so it seemed, Demon found himself floating in a grey place, with a myriad silver stars whirling in a night sky that shimmered and changed in dizzying swirls. This was definitely not his normal sort of dream. Black sand stretched below him as far as his eyes could see, and on the horizon there were two huge arches, one bone-white, one golden-brown.

Suddenly a shadowy dot appeared through the white arch, very far away, but rapidly coming closer, resolving itself into a strange being, all long, thin arms and legs, and eyes like pools of deep water. In its hand it carried a torch of black and gold flame.

"Pandemonius!" said the god, sounding surprised. "How did you get here?"

Quickly, Demon explained how he'd used the dreamcatcher. Then he told Morpheus about Fenrir.

"I think he's having terrible nightmares," he finished, "and you were the only one I could think of who might be able to help."

"Very well," said Morpheus. "But don't use the dreamcatcher in that way again. It's not meant to contact me. I'll have to fix that. This is a dangerous place to be. Anything you think here can become real."

Morpheus took the black crystal and made a twisty gesture with his torch, and then Demon knew nothing more till he woke the next morning with the crystal lying on his chest. On the floor by his bed, written in flowing letters of black sand, was a message.

THE WOLF DREAMS WELL NOW . . . M.

Demon was just pouring a big load of Sun Cow dung down the poo chute, to the appreciative roars of the hundred-armed monsters beneath, when Arnie the griffin landed beside him in a flurry of golden feathers.

"Hey, Pan's scrawny kid, old Heffy wants to see you quick smart. I should run, if I was you. He sounded as if he'd got his beard in quite a twist about something."

Demon left his barrow tipped on its side, and started to run up the rocky mountain path to Hephaestus's forge at once. He had a bad feeling right down to his toes. Heffy didn't usually get bothered about things — he was quite calm for a god, really. What could have gone wrong? Had

Colin the Colchian Dragon eaten
something that made it gassy again?
Was the whole of Olympus about
to blow up?

Puffing and panting, Demon hurtled
into the forge to find the smith god
kneeling in front of the wall, where
a large flashing red gemstone was
making a horrible wailing sound. Colin
the Colchian Dragon was curled into
an enormous purple ball with its tail
wrapped around its head.

"What's THAT?" Demon shouted,
putting his fingers in his ears.

"The Typhon alarm," Hephaestus
yelled back. "I'm trying to turn it off!"
He raised a huge, grimy fist and gave it
a wallop. Suddenly there was a blissful

27

quiet, although the jewel was still flashing red.

"Who's Typhon?" Demon asked into the silence, as the Colchian Dragon uncurled itself with a rattle of scales.

Hephaestus sighed, tugging on his beard, which was indeed messier than usual.

"He's a terrible hundred-headed monster," said the smith god. "Zeus put me in charge of him. He's been asleep under a mountain for the last thousand years, but that alarm tells me he's waking up for some reason. I need to go and see what's up – and you're coming with me, Pandemonius. Every one of Typhon's heads is some sort of animal – bears, lions, dragons, that sort of thing

– so I've a feeling we'll need those pipes of yours."

"Can I come too?" asked Colin. "I haven't been out for ages, and I've cried out LOTS of fire jewels for you." The dragon looked sideways at Demon. "And I helped you with your display for the gods of the North, too," it said.

"Oh, very well," said Hephaestus. "But we'll have to borrow Helios's sun boat. You're too big to travel on the Iris Express now."

A short while later, Demon, Hephaestus and the Colchian Dragon were aboard a huge golden boat, round as a bowl, with one big oar at the back. Demon had his medicine bag, his pipes and four enormous bags of charcoal for the dragon in case it got hungry. He'd left the magic medicine box in Heffy's forge, as it needed mending after it had tried and failed to crush an ice diamond in Asgard.

"Now," said the smith god. "Let's see if I remember how this thing works." Hephaestus wiggled the oar left, then right, and with a jerk, the sun boat shot up into the sky. Higher and higher they went, until the air turned cold and dark as the boat lurched from side to side, banging into stars along the way.

"By Zeus's ears," said Hephaestus, wrestling with the oar, which seemed to have a mind of its own, "I think this wretched contraption needs a steering modification."

Tiny chips of bright silver stardust fell into the boat, clinking and tinkling, then flickering out and turning black. Colin nibbled on them.

"Tasty!" the dragon said. "Like charcoal but with a hint of sky."

Clinging on to the side to keep from being thrown out, Demon scooped some of the stardust into a wide-necked bottle. He'd show it to Chiron, his centaur teacher, and find out if it could be used as medicine, he thought. But before the bottle was more than half full, Hephaestus gave a yell, wrenching the oar over to his right.

"Star Nymphs, ahoy!" he shouted. "Watch out! Boat coming through!" Suddenly, there was a tremendous bang,

and all at once the sun boat was full of
thrashing limbs, angry screams and the
faint smell of deep cold, tinged with
flowers.

"Oof!" said Demon as someone
landed on him, knocking him backwards
into the Colchian Dragon, which roared
angrily and let out a belch of purple
flame. Everything was chaos for a
few minutes, as the boat veered and
rocked, nearly tipping over. Eventually
Hephaestus got it back under control.

As the boat resumed its progress
through the sky, Demon saw that the
thrashing limbs and angry screams
belonged to six nymphs, their floaty
robes silver against the gold of the
boat. Each had a crown of living stars
whirling around her head, and together

they shone so brightly that Demon had to squint to see them properly. The smallest of them was standing in front of Hephaestus, shaking one long finger at him.

"Careless, clumsy oaf of a god!" she shrieked. "Take us back at once! How dare you kidnap us like this?"

Hephaestus looked embarrassed.

"Now, now, Maia," he said. "It was an accident. This wretched sun boat of Helios's isn't easy to steer, you know."

"She always gets so angry," said a voice in Demon's ear. It was the nymph who had fallen on him. "I'm Alcyone, by the way. One of the seven Pleiades, you know. Sorry if I squashed you."

"Nice to meet you," said Demon. "I'm Demon." Then he frowned, counting noses. "But there are only six of you."

Alcyone laughed.

"Oh, Electra's invisible. She's here, but she's rather shy." Her eyes twinkled. "She's looking at you right now. I think she might like you."

Demon blushed. He wasn't at all sure about an invisible nymph admirer.

3

Terrible Typhon

The rest of the journey was taken up
by quite a lot of arguing, and more
shouting, as each of the six visible
Pleiades in turn tried to persuade
Hephaestus to turn back. Demon spent
the time trying to calm Colin the
Colchian Dragon down.

"This was supposed to be a nice
treat," the dragon moaned. "All
this crossness can't be good for my
digestion. I'll turn red, and it'll all start
again, you see if it doesn't. I'm sure I
can feel the gas building up now."

"You won't turn red, and I'm sure your stomach will be fine," Demon said soothingly. "Have some of this nice charcoal, and then you can clean up the stardust so nobody slips on it." He tipped half a sack of charcoal down the dragon's throat, and soon it was munching and mumbling contentedly. Despite its size, and its windy worries, it was really a beast of simple needs.

"BE QUIET, ALL OF YOU!" Hephaestus roared finally as the nymphs reached a fever pitch. "OR I'LL SEND YOU TO APHRODITE!"

There was a small silence.

"Oh, please don't," said Alcyone. "You know how we hate being her nymphs-in-waiting. She's so very . . . well . . .

pink and fluffy. But we really do need to be back in our part of the sky soon, or everything will get in a terrible muddle. The stars do wander so, and if we're not there to herd them back into place all the Earth humans in their ships will get terribly confused."

"Where are we going anyway?" Maia butted in.

By the time Hephaestus had explained about the Typhon alarm, the boat was swooping low over the sea. Beneath them lay a large island, shaped like a wonky dog's head, with a mountain just where the dog's ear would be. Large boulders flew up into the air around the mountain, raining down onto the ground, which shook with the impact. There was a huge hole in the top that seemed to be getting bigger as they watched. The mountain was also roaring so loudly that, even with his fingers in his ears, Demon could feel the sound through his whole body, as if it was being buffeted by an enormous wind. He saw Hephaestus's mouth move, but couldn't tell what he was saying.

"Take us out of range!" Demon yelled at the smith god, but he couldn't even hear his own words, so he pointed upwards instead, hoping Heffy would understand. Immediately the sun boat swooped towards the heavens again, leaving the dreadful racket behind.

"Well," said the smith god. "I think it's safe to say that Typhon's awake. But how are we going to put him back to sleep? He'll never hear those pipes of yours, Pandemonius." Hephaestus turned to the star nymphs. "You lot sing, don't you?"

Maia nodded.

"Well, yes," she said. "We sing to soothe the stars when they get cross. But I don't see how . . ."

"Sing then," Hephaestus commanded the nymphs. "Sing for all you're worth." And he turned the boat downwards again.

It wasn't so much a song, Demon thought, as the Pleiades opened their mouths, as a sound like the chiming of a thousand silvery bells. But as soon as they got close to Typhon again, it was completely drowned out. The hole in the top of the mountain was even bigger now, and out of it poked at least forty beast heads of all types on very long necks, with more appearing every minute. Demon recognised dragons, bulls, snakes, wolves and griffins, but there were a lot more than that, and they all looked dreadfully scary. Each head was a hundred times the size of the actual animal, and each was clearly furious. Hephaestus steered the boat upwards again hurriedly, as several of the snake heads lunged at them.

"He's nearly free!" the god yelled when they could hear again. "We have to do something fast! Zeus will be furious if Typhon escapes!"

Demon shuddered. He didn't want to

be anywhere near a furious Zeus. Then his eyes fell on the Colchian Dragon. The beast was curled into a shivering ball and the back half of it had turned bright red with fear. An idea flicked into his mind. It was a very dangerous idea, but it was the only thing he could come up with.

"Do you think a dragon fart might stun Typhon long enough for me to play my pipes?" he asked slowly.

Hephaestus's mouth fell open, and the Pleiades all let out tiny shrieks of horror.

"Noooo!" moaned the dragon. "Don't make me. Must. Keep. It. In. Mustkeepitin. Mustkeepitinmustkeepitinmustkeepitin!"

Demon stroked Colin's purple head gently.

"Just the one," he said. "I promise you can have all the charcoal right afterwards to turn you purple again. And I'll never ever ask you to do it again."

Hephaestus scratched his head with one grimy finger.

"I don't know, young Pandemonius," he said. "It's very risky. What if there's a spark from somewhere? It could blow us all to kingdom come."

"And think of the smell!" all the star nymphs chorused, holding their noses.

"Oh, the shame, the terrible shame!"

the dragon groaned, curling itself into an even smaller ball of red and purple misery.

Demon scrambled to his feet, making the boat rock.

"If we don't do something soon, Typhon will be free, and I for one don't want to face Zeus's wrath. Do you?" he asked.

Hephaestus glared at him but Demon didn't back down, and after a short pause, they all shook their heads, even the dragon.

"Right, then," Demon said, delving into his medicine bag. "Let's do this. Luckily I've got a whole lot of Chiron's special masks in here. Put them on."

"Ordering me about," Hephaestus grumbled, as he fitted the mask of cotton and reeds to his hairy face with one hand. "Those gods of the north gave you too much freedom, I reckon. What happened to all those nice manners?"

Down they went again into the maelstrom of noise. Demon helped the dragon to position its bottom over the edge of the boat, draping its tail out of the way, and as Hephaestus steered as close as he could to Typhon's gnashing, roaring heads, the dragon squeezed its eyes shut, aimed and let out an enormous blast of gas.

Immediately the animal heads were shrouded in a hazy cloud of noxious green. Shortly afterwards, the roars turned to chokes, and then silence fell. Zooming even closer, Hephaestus took the sun boat down to hover just above the huge hole in the mountain. Through the haze they could see Typhon's many heads slumped on the edge of the hole.

"Mmphrm pmphrm?" Hephaestus asked, his voice muffled by the mask. Demon turned from helping the dragon down from the edge of the boat.

"Whmph?" he said, as he poured three bags of charcoal down its eager throat, avoiding the very sharp rows of teeth. The star nymphs were all fanning the green smoke away with little moans of dismay.

The smith god pointed urgently to where Demon's pipes stuck out of his tunic, and then to where one of Typhon's heads was beginning to stir. Demon pulled them out, about to put them to his lips when he realised the problem. How was he going to play them with his mask on?

The smith god must have realised at the same time. Reaching down, he picked up one of the charcoal bags and began to flap it very fast. The green haze around the boat disappeared, just as Demon heard a small roar from below, and then another. He'd have to risk it. If Typhon woke up, all the dragon's work would have been for nothing.

Taking a deep breath, Demon ripped

off the mask and put the pipes to his lips, blowing Pan's special twiddle notes for all he was worth. The roars stopped again immediately, and as he peered over the edge of the sun boat, all Typhon's heads, eyes closed and sleeping, slithered back down into the ground and disappeared.

Just then, the dragon got hiccups from eating the charcoal too fast. It hicced out one tiny purple-blue spark, which floated over the side of the boat and then downwards. With a different kind of roar, the green gas exploded instantly, sending the boat spiralling upwards, rocking from side to side and out of control. Underneath them, the hole in the top of the mountain fell in on itself, boulders bouncing and bounding down the sides, until all that was left was a small round depression in the ground.

Hephaestus wrestled with the steering oar for all he was worth, and eventually the sun boat was back under his control. Though everyone was tumbled and mussed and bruised, they all cheered as they sped high over the sea and away from Typhon's prison.

"Well done, Colin," said Demon, as the dragon munched on more of its charcoal, slowly turning purple again.

"Double extra rations for you when we get back to the forge," said Hephaestus, grinning, as the star nymphs crowded round it, patting its scaly flanks.

4

Notes from Nowhere

"Whoa!" said the smith god suddenly, pointing downwards. "What's that? I'm sure it wasn't here when we came by before." Demon and the star nymphs all rushed to the side of the sun boat, making it tip dangerously.

Two enormous pillars of rock loomed up out of the land beneath, one on either side of the sea. Clouds of grey dust hung about the pillars as they shifted and settled, rumbling slightly.

"I don't remember seeing them before

either," said Maia. "How could they have got there?"

"I don't know," Hephaestus said slowly. "But you can be sure I'll make it my business to find out. I think we've discovered where the disturbance that woke Typhon came from."

"Look!" said Alcyone softly, poking Demon in the ribs. At first Demon couldn't see anything, but then, as they flew past, he noticed a tiny figure striding away southwards from the mess. It was a figure he thought he recognised, though he'd only seen it once before, in the Desert of Burning Sand.

"Horrible Heracles!" he muttered. "I bet you he caused all this." He was about to tell Hephaestus, when all the star nymphs screamed at once.

"Oh no!" Maia yelled, looking up into the heavens. "I knew this would happen. The stars are wandering out of position. Take us back quick, Hephaestus."

Demon felt a brush of something against his back as he stared up at the jumble of stars, which had gathered in a large, glittery group in the centre of the sky, and then the Pleiades all started to sing. Louder and louder their silvery voices got, as the sun boat headed into the emptiness of the heavens, and Demon sat down, leaning against the warm bulk of the Colchian Dragon again, and drifted off to sleep listening to the nymphs' soothing melody.

★

A long time later, Demon woke to a rough hand shaking his shoulder.

"Out you get, young Pandemonius," Hephaestus said. "I left you to sleep while I gave that box of yours a quick upgrade. We're home, and now I have to clean this boat out before I return it to Helios. It's all over stardust and charcoal."

"I'll help," Demon mumbled, but Hephaestus shook his head.

"Me and Colin will do it," he said. "That dragon's all purple and perky now, he needs a job. You get off to bed. You've got a lot of poo-shovelling to do tomorrow, I expect." The smith god ruffled Demon's curly hair. "And find your manners again, young Stablemaster. If you try ordering the other gods about like you did to me today, you'll find yourself turned into a burnt honeycake or worse, I shouldn't wonder."

As Demon stumbled sleepily down the mountain towards the stables, he couldn't help wishing for a bit of peace. He'd had a lot of adventures lately, and all he wanted was to spend some time quietly with his beasts.

"And I've got homework from Chiron to catch up with, too," he grumbled to himself. Chiron was his centaur teacher, and lived down on Earth in a cave on Mount Pelion. He was also the greatest healer who'd ever lived. Climbing slowly up to his loft, Demon was just about

to fall into bed and go to sleep again,
when he saw a bit of paper lying on his
bed. It was very mangled around the
edges, with strange, uneven holes on
one side.

"What in the name of Zeus's big
toenail?" he said out loud, picking up
the paper and opening it. It was sticky,
as if somebody or something had
drooled on it. In glowing green-gold
letters, it said:

Come quickly!
Unicorn emergency!

Wiping his damp hand on his tunic, he
went over to Bion's side of the loft and
shook him awake.

"What's this?" he asked the bleary-eyed faun. "Where did it come from, and who's it from? Is there a problem with Unicorn I don't know about?"

Bion shook his head, yawning.

"Dunno," he said. "It was there when I came to bed. Nobody came to the stables to deliver it. Unicorn was fine last night when I checked."

Demon ran down the stairs again, wide awake now. He rushed over to Unicorn's stall at the far end, but she was curled up and fast asleep, tiny, whiffling snores coming from her nostrils. Opening the door very gently, he tiptoed in, careful not to wake her. Unicorns didn't like boys very much, so normally the nymphs looked after her and milked her when Aphrodite needed her weekly bath.

Unicorn milk was very good for beautiful skin, according to the goddess.

Holding his breath, Demon checked her shining horn and flanks and legs for damage, but he could see nothing that was in any way an emergency. Backing away carefully, he felt for the door behind him. A large splinter ran into his thumb.

"Ouch!" he said, without thinking.

Unicorn's eyes, blue as a summer sky, flicked open.

"Aargh!" the beast scream-whinnied. "A boy-hoy-hoy in my stable! A nasty, dirty boy-hoy-hoy!" Scrambling to her feet and lowering her horn, Unicorn charged.

Demon whipped round and ran, slamming the door shut behind him. The horn came through the bars, scraping hard along the side of his scalp. It hurt. A lot. And what felt like a whole river of blood was now running down beside his ear. Immediately, Offy and Yukus, the two magical healing snakes who lived round his neck as a golden necklace, flashed into action, mending the wound.

'Thanks, boys," he said shakily, once he had retreated to a safe distance.

"It wasss our pleasssure," said the snakes, settling back round his neck again.

Demon sat down on a bale of sun hay to recover. Suddenly, there was a rustle nearby, and the scent of something he thought he recognised. The hairs on the back of his neck prickled, as if someone was watching him.

"Who's there?" he called. But there was no reply, and he could see no one.

"What's up, Pan's scrawny kid?" growled a sleepy griffin voice. "What are you making such a racket for? You're ruining my beauty kip. Shut up or I'll have Demon leg for my breakfast."

"Never mind," Demon said, as he climbed back up to the loft. "Go back to sleep, Arnie. It'll keep till morning."

Demon didn't sleep very well. Nightmares of unicorns with broken legs, unicorns with purple spots and, worst of all, unicorn skeletons, kept waking him up. As Eos drew back the pink curtains of dawn, he jumped out of bed, and grabbed the note, stuffing it inside his tunic. Until he knew who had sent it, he couldn't do much about it, though, and it was bothering him. The thought of any animal in pain was not something he was ever happy about.

The stables below were full of the noise of waking beasts, yawning, stretching and in some cases clamouring for their morning ambrosia cake. Doris the Hydra was particularly affectionate, drooling mightily and rubbing its nine heads against him as the buckets of food were tipped into its manger. Behind Demon came Bion with the poo barrow and shovel, and between them they had the stables spick and span in almost no time at all.

"Right!" said Demon, when they were finished. "Listen up, you lot. Did anyone come with a note for me yesterday?"

Anyone else would have heard a whole lot of animal noises. But Demon could speak every beast language. All he heard was a whole lot of NO. He didn't think he'd better go near Unicorn again, so he stepped outside and had a word with his friend, the nymph, Althea.

"Can you ask Unicorn if she knows anything about this, please?" he asked her, showing her the note. The nymph's nose wrinkled as she touched it.

"Ugh! All slobbery," Althea said. "And

who writes in glowy ink now? That's so last year." But she agreed to ask. When the nymph came back, she was shaking her head.

"Unicorn doesn't know anything about it. She hasn't seen her family for years, so now she's very worried. Oh, and she said to tell you to have a bath because you stink of poo!" With that she ran off to polish some flowers with the rest of her sisters. A tiny, silvery giggle rang out behind Demon, but was quickly cut off as he whipped round, glaring.

"It's not funn . . ." he said, his voice trailing off, as he realised there was nobody there. Demon scratched his head. Must have imagined it, he thought. But the hairs on his neck still prickled as if invisible eyes were watching him.

5

Canine Chaos

Feeling worried and out of sorts, Demon trailed over to Melanie the Naiad's spring. She was sitting in the cup of a giant purple waterlily, combing her long blue locks with a silver comb.

"Do I really smell bad?" he asked.

Melanie sniffed carefully.

"No more than usual," she said. "But you can have a swim and a wash in my pool, if you like? I'll even lend you my new soap if you tell me all about your adventures in Asgard."

Demon eyed her. "Do you swear not to look while I'm bathing?" he asked.

"Pinky promise," she said, holding out her little finger.

A little while later, just as he'd finished telling Melanie all about Ratatosk the squirrel, and how wicked Loki the trickster and the dark elves had kidnapped him, he heard the sound of loud barking. Melanie tutted as he hastily dried off and got into a clean tunic.

"That Golden Dog is so noisy," she said. "I don't know how poor old Amaltheia puts up with him." Golden

Dog was a mysterious creature, who lived in the stables with his best friend, the ancient nanny goat who had looked after Zeus when he was little.

Demon cocked his head listening.

"That's not Golden," he said. "Or at least, it's not only him . . ." Before Demon could say another word, a pack of hounds came racing out of thin air, led by Golden Dog. They were white and very hairy, with their red ears pricked up, and long tails wagging frantically.

"Demon!" they barked, crowding round him, and jumping up to put their huge paws on his shoulders. "We found you! We hunted you down! She will be pleased!"

Golden Dog was doing his usual leaping and licking, swiping his long pink tongue over both Demon and Melanie until the naiad screeched.

"Off! Off! Get away from my pool, you wretched beasts!"

Melanie grabbed some clumps of floating waterweed and flung them at the hounds who had leapt into the water and were cavorting around in her spring like puppies.

Demon hid a smile. Dogs were always so enthusiastic. Then his brain caught up with what he'd just heard.

"Wait!" he said to a particularly playful hound, who was licking his clean toes. "Who will be pleased? Did you deliver me a note last night?" But the dogs weren't listening to him. They leapt out of the pool, shaking streams of water everywhere, and raced into the stables. Demon heard an ominous clatter, and raced after them, but it was too late.

Brooms and buckets lay scattered everywhere. Bion the faun had fallen smack on his face into the poo barrow, and poor Doris the Hydra lay on its back, green legs kicking in the air, with wet pawprints all over it.

Before Demon could even open his mouth to shout he heard a strangled squawk, and Arnie the griffin came bounding past, wings flapping, with the whole pack of dogs on his heels.

"Save me, Pan's scrawny kid," Arnie gasped, orange eyes wide with fear, which was most unlike the normally fierce griffin.

"STOP!" Demon yelled as he ran after them. "You dogs come back here! Come to heel!"

But as Arnie soared into the air, with a leaping hound just missing the griffin's lion's tail by a hair, the pack streaked away around Olympus, howling their heads off.

Demon knew he'd never catch them. Right now there weren't any animals outside for them to chase, so he turned back to the stables to survey the damage. Doris the Hydra was back on its feet, whimpering a little and shaking its nine heads, and Bion had climbed out of the poo barrow and was spitting clumps of straw – and other more unmentionable things – out of his mouth.

"Are you both all right?" Demon asked.

"I'm fine," Bion said, though he looked a bit pale.

Doris just tottered over and nuzzled Demon affectionately. "More snackies?" it asked hopefully.

Demon caught a flash of yellow out of the corner of his eye, as he started to pick things up and set the stables to rights.

"Come here, Golden Dog," he said sternly. "Who were those hounds, and why did you bring them here? They could have killed poor Arnie and Doris. What were you thinking?"

"Yes, you tell him, young Golden," came a bleaty voice from a nearby stall. "Why, those wretched creatures made such a racket it nearly turned my milk sour." It was old Amaltheia the nanny goat.

Demon had never seen Golden Dog look so guilty before. The big animal slunk out, tail between his legs and ears back, creeping to Demon's feet on low legs.

"Sorry, Demon," he whined, as Demon heard faint nymph and cherub shrieks from outside. "I brought one of them last night to help deliver Artemis's message, and he told the others it smelled so good in here that they all wanted to come and fetch you. I didn't think they'd go crazy like that."

Demon felt as if he'd been kicked in the belly by a centaur.

"Wait," he said slowly. "Did you just say that the unicorn message was from ARTEMIS?"

Golden Dog's ears pricked up.

"Yes! Yes!" he barked, wagging his tail. "From Artemis! She wants to see you quite badly. Those hounds are hers."

Demon groaned. The last time he'd seen the goddess of the hunt, she had threatened to shoot him with her silver bow. Only Hestia the kitchen goddess had been able to stop her. He should have realised the hounds belonged to Artemis.

What on earth could Artemis want with him now? Demon shivered slightly as he remembered hearing the gossip about poor Actaeon, who'd seen the goddess bathing in a moonlit pool one night by mistake. Artemis had turned him into a white stag and had her hounds hunt him down and tear him to pieces. She was definitely not one of the safer goddesses to tangle with, but if she wanted him, he'd have to go. Demon sighed.

"I'd better go and find those hounds," he said.

Demon had never said *It's not my fault* so many times to so many cross nymphs and cherubs. Artemis's hounds had left a trail of destruction all round Olympus, knocking off flowers, nipping nymphs and chasing cherubs up trees.

"It'll take us ages to grow all the blossom back," said an angry Ophelia, the dryad in charge of the orchards.

Finally, Demon tracked the hounds down to the poo chute, where they were licking up the remains of the last barrowload, and even worse, rolling in it. He could hear the hundred-armed monsters below roaring with annoyance.

"Disgusting creatures," Demon said. "Bad dogs! Come here at once and stop eating that. It'll make you sick."

The largest hound looked up and gave him a doggy grin, smelly smears of brown and green coating its neck.

"But it's so delicious," it barked.

"I don't care," said Demon. "I need to know what this unicorn emergency is, and why Artemis wants me."

At the goddess's name, immediately all the hounds sat to attention.

"Artemis! Artemis! Artemis!" they howled, all on different notes, so it blended together like a song. "Beloved Artemis!"

Demon shook his head. He knew a losing battle when he saw one.

"STAY!" he said in his sternest voice, walking towards the stables again. Then he sniffed as a waft of poo-laden air drifted past. "You smell really bad," he muttered.

When the hounds had stopped howling, Demon returned carrying his medicine sack and the newly upgraded magic medicine box, and with Golden Dog for company.

"Take me to Artemis," he said, clutching Golden's collar as the hounds crowded round him, whacking him with the frantic wagging of their long tails. "Let's see what this unicorn emergency is all about."

As they left, Demon thought he felt a small hand clutch onto his tunic, but he forgot it almost immediately as he felt the whirling, stomach-churning sensation that meant Golden Dog was taking him through the little gaps in time and space.

When it stopped, Demon opened his eyes. He was in a glade that smelt of pine trees and ancient green things. A shining goddess was standing before him, and Golden Dog had disappeared.

6

Artemis Awaits

Artemis was dressed in a knee-length
white tunic, clasped at the shoulder
with a circular silver brooch in the
shape of two running stags. In her hand
she carried a silver bow, with a quiver
of silver arrows slung over her back,
and her feet were shod in silver sandals
whose ribbons twined up her long legs
like growing vines. She smelled of
moonlight and violets and fresh blood.

Demon fell to his knees, and then flat
on his face, as soon as he saw her. One
of those silver-shod feet was tapping

angrily on the grass, and Artemis was frowning. This was never a good sign in Demon's experience. A frowning goddess could only lead to one thing. Visions of a large, smoking heap of Demon-shaped charcoal flashed through his head.

"Where have you been, Stablemaster?" Artemis asked, and her voice was both as loud as the belling of a hundred packs of hounds, and as soft as a breeze through trees at night. "You have kept me waiting."

"I-I'm s-sorry, Your M-moonlight Magnificence," he stammered. "I was away with Hephaestus, there was—"

Artemis's foot inserted itself under Demon's jaw, closing his mouth so his words were cut off.

"The smith god's affairs do not concern me," she said, and her tone bit into him as harshly as a giant fire ant. "Only my own. Now get up and face me. I have work for you to do."

As Demon scrambled to his feet, the hounds crowded round the goddess, rubbing their big hairy heads against her and whining with pleasure as she bent down to pull their long, red ears and pat them, speaking to each by name. *Surely a goddess who loves her dogs so much can't be all bad?* Demon thought.

He looked round at where he was. Tall pine trees soared overhead, their needles soft under his feet. In the sky above, a crescent moon shone among the stars like a shining sliver of cut fingernail. Demon had just enough time to wonder if the Pleiades had managed to herd all the stars back into their right places, when Artemis straightened up from her hounds.

"What do you know about healing unicorns?" she asked abruptly.

Demon thought about lying, but he knew she'd only find him out.

"Not m-much, Your Silvery Serenity," he admitted. "The unicorn on Olympus has never been sick, and I haven't come across any others." He eyed the goddess cautiously and decided to risk a question. "What's wrong with your unicorn, if you don't mind me asking?"

Artemis frowned again, but this time Demon thought it was with worry.

"It's not just one unicorn, Stablemaster. It's my whole herd. All the wild unicorns on Earth, in fact. The adult mares are very sick indeed, and some of the foals are near death, though the stallions are fighting it hard."

Artemis glared at Demon, her silver-grey eyes flashing in the dim light. "Can you cure them?"

Demon's heart sank. One sick unicorn was bad enough, but a whole herd? That was going to be almost impossible. He fingered the side of his head where he'd been gored. However was he going to get near them if they felt the same about boys as the unicorn on Olympus did?

"I-I'll do my very best, Your A-amazing

Archeriness," he said, backing away
till he bumped into the rough trunk of
a pine tree. "But I'll have to see them
first."

Artemis took two gliding steps
towards him and seized his chin in one
long-fingered hand.

"You will cure them, Pandemonius,"
she whispered, as softly as moonlight
falling on ice. "If one unicorn dies, I will
give you to my hounds to hunt and then
let them tear you to pieces one inch at
a time. Are you going to fail me?"

Demon thought of poor Actaeon's
fate again, and shook his head
frantically. The hounds crowded round
him, all barking together, and he began
to tremble. Were they going to eat a

bit of him now, as a warning not to fail? He squeezed his eyes shut, hoping that maybe it wouldn't hurt too much.

But then something wonderfully unexpected happened. Demon began to listen to what the hounds were saying.

"We LIKE Demon!" they howled.

"He's one of us!"

"We won't hurt him!"

Artemis stamped her foot, and the ground trembled.

"YOU WILL IF I SAY SO," she roared. Pine needles showered down around Demon's head like fragrant raindrops. Then Artemis spoke again, more softly.

"And if you won't, my hounds, I shall encase him in one of these pines for all eternity, and let the bears and boars use him for a scratching post."

Demon began to tremble again when he saw several tall figures step out of the surrounding trees. Literally out of them. These were not anything like his orchard friend Ophelia the dryad, up on Olympus. They were tall and green and fierce-looking, and they surrounded the goddess.

"Our pine trees will not take him, Moon Lady, nor will any of the trees of our sisters," said the tallest. "Do not threaten the son of Pan."

"No," said a deep, velvety voice, like mossy bark on ancient trees. "Do not threaten Pandemonius in my forests, Artemis. I will not allow it." A tall figure with thick, hairy goat legs stepped out between the trees.

Demon let out a gusty sigh of relief. His dad had arrived!

"Pan!" Artemis spat. "You interfering old goat. I'll do what I like."

But Pan shook his curly, bearded head and his yellow eyes with their slitted black pupils narrowed.

"My son is a good boy and a good healer," Pan said. "It's time you Olympians showed him some respect. Most of you threaten him and treat him like dirt, but who do you turn to when one of your precious beasts is sick? Has he ever let any of you down?"

Demon's heart swelled, and he felt tears prick at the back of his eyes. His dad had neglected him for most of his life. In fact, he'd never even met the forest god till he came and whisked Demon away to the Stables of the Gods. But it seemed his dad had been noticing things after all. And now he was here, standing up for him against Zeus's own daughter.

Artemis threw up her hands.

"Oh, very well," she said. "Since you all seem to think so much of the boy, I'll be nice. And anyway, I'm sure he'll cure my unicorns, so none of it will be necessary anyway."

Pan laughed, striding over to lift Demon up into his familiar godhug that smelled of pungent green things, goaty musk and old, stale blood.

"Of course he will," the forest god chuckled. "Won't you, my boy?"

"Y-yes, Your Dadness," Demon said breathlessly. Pan's hugs were always very rib-squeezing.

"Right then," said Pan. "Now that's settled, I'll be off. I promised your mother I'd drop in on her and the twins and I'm already late."

With that, Pan disappeared into the trees as if he'd never been there. The dryads slipped back into their pines, and then it was just Demon, Artemis

and the hounds in the glade once more.
Demon had a hollow feeling just below
his ribs. For a minute he wished his dad
had taken him along. Although he knew
his mum was happy with her new babies,
he still missed her sometimes.

Then, in the quiet stillness Pan and
the dryads had left behind, the hair
on the nape of his neck prickled, just
as it had back on Olympus. Suddenly
Demon felt a breath on his cheek that
shouldn't have been there. Whirling
round, he looked behind him, but there
was nobody to be seen.

"No need to be so jumpy,
Pandemonius," said Artemis. "I said
I'd be nice."

"I-it's not you, Your Moonlight

87

Magnificence," he said. "I just thought
. . . well, I just thought someone
else was here. But I must have been
mistaken."

Artemis laughed. "Maybe there
is, maybe there isn't," she said
mysteriously. "But come, there is no
more time to waste. Bring your things
and follow me. My unicorns are waiting."

With a cry like a horn blowing, she
ran out of the glade, the hounds loping
behind her like white smoke.

7

Goddess Girl Power

Demon had never found it so hard to keep up with someone. He ran behind the goddess and her hounds, deeper and deeper into the wild, untamed forest. The medicine sack over his shoulder and the magic medicine box under his arm became heavier and heavier.

Suddenly the magic medicine box lit up and began to flash red.

"Shaking overload," it said in its tinny, metallic voice. "Initiating emergency travel mode. High risk of battery drain. Do you want to proceed?"

"Yes," Demon gasped. "Whatever you think is best." What did 'high risk of battery drain' even mean anyway? He had no idea. The box was always talking in silly jargon he couldn't understand, and he knew better than to complain. It would sulk and refuse to help him at all if he did.

As the box began to shrink, Demon nearly dropped it. Soon it was so small that he could carry it in the palm of his hand.

"Why have you never done that before?" he panted crossly. "You know you're so heavy my arm nearly falls off every time I have to carry you. Is this part of Heffy's new upgrade?" But the box didn't reply, so he tucked it into his tunic, beside his precious Pan pipes. *I hope it'll unshrink itself when we get wherever we're going,* he thought. The box had proven temperamental in the past, and he didn't trust it not to let him down again.

As Demon ran on, the worry about how he was going to approach the unicorns raised itself again. What if they wouldn't let him near them? Artemis had promised his dad she'd be nice, but goddesses were notorious for being fickle. She could still change her mind if Demon couldn't cure her herd.

Soon, though, Demon had no room for any thoughts in his head. He was concentrating too hard on putting one running foot in front of the other. His breath came in long, panting gasps, and he had to keep rubbing the sweat out of his eyes with his free hand. The medicine sack in his other hand was beginning to rub where he'd slung it over his shoulder, and he could feel a blister forming.

"Wait!" he tried to shout, but his throat was too dry. Up ahead, Artemis shouted something, but Demon couldn't hear what she said, and it was at that moment that he ran into something. Something that slammed into his middle like a hot, bouncy wire. With an oof of pain, he was flung backwards onto the ground, completely winded.

It was almost a relief to be still, but the feeling didn't last for long. Something dropped onto his stomach from a tree. Something with too many skittery, hairy legs. Another dropped, and another, onto his head and his calves. Demon screamed hoarsely as the things began to wrap him in sticky fibres, turning him over and over so fast that he became dizzy.

"Artemis! Help!" he whispered, as he heard the hounds baying somewhere away in the distance. But he knew the goddess couldn't hear him.

Was it spiders that had taken him? As the spinning and wrapping sensations came to a dizzying halt, Demon tried to stop panicking long enough to look properly at his captors, but it was hard in the faint moonlight. He could see round bodies, and the glitter of huge, many-faceted eyes. Spiders for sure

. . . but then he squinted. Were those wings? Demon thought of all the winged creatures he knew, but none of them fitted. Then, quite suddenly, he felt himself being lifted upwards. He tried to struggle, but he was held too tightly in his sticky bonds.

As they soared above the treetops, Demon turned his head as much as he could. What he saw then made all his limbs freeze solid with fear. He had definitely been taken by enormous spiders . . . but they had bat wings! He did love all creatures, but spiders were probably his least favourite. It was just something about the way all those legs scuttled . . .

Over the rush of the wind Demon could now hear high, squeaking voices, but he couldn't make out what they were saying. Insect language had never been something he understood easily. What did the spider-bats want with him? Were they going to eat him? He couldn't get a hand free to get at his pipes, and even if he had, putting the spider-bats to sleep while they were all flying through the air didn't seem like such a good plan.

All at once, they were swooping down into the forest again. Thin pine branches flicked against Demon's face and body, stinging him, but he could do nothing to fend them off.

As the spider-bats laid him on the ground, he struggled again.

"Let me go," he yelled, but the creatures just chittered at him, clicking their legs. Demon shuddered. Why did they have to have so many? He closed his eyes and waited for the biting to start.

But it didn't. Instead, something wet and warm swiped across his forehead.

"Arrgh!" Demon spluttered, his eyes springing open again.

He was surrounded by hairy white heads, which licked his face mercilessly with long, pink tongues.

"Demon! Demon! Demon!" they barked, as the spider-bats soared up among the trees.

Now Demon was totally confused – and rather cross.

"Gerroff me!" he ordered, as several pairs of heavy hound paws dug into his chest.

Then Artemis was there, raising a sharp silver arrowhead to slice through his bonds as the hounds retreated and the spider-bats flew higher into the trees, and landed, flipping upside down to hang on the branches.

"What just happened?" he demanded, when he had scrambled to his feet, too angry to remember his manners.

Artemis shrugged, a little smile playing at the corner of her mouth.

"You were being a proper slowcoach, stumbling along behind me like a tortoise, so I got my little flying friends to give you a ride. What are you complaining about?"

Demon opened his mouth, then closed it again as he saw the steely glint in the goddess's eyes. He knew perfectly well she'd done it on purpose to frighten him.

"Now," said Artemis, picking sticky bits off her arrow. "You can't go into the unicorns like that. They don't like boys. I'll have to transform you into a girl."

This time Demon's mouth dropped open with shock and stayed that way.

Artemis laughed.

"How did you think you were going to enter unicorn lands?" she asked. "I thought you were the beast expert.

Don't you know the unicorns won't allow a boy to touch them?"

Demon found his voice with difficulty.

"I-I did know that, Your Shining Serenity," he said. "I was a bit worried about it, to be honest. But how . . .?" He gestured down at himself. "I mean – I AM a boy."

Artemis shook her head.

"Not while you're in there," she said, pointing far up ahead to a band of lavender mist across the pathway. Making a doorway with one tiny flick of her hands, she pulled things out of the air faster than Demon's eyes could see. Soon there was a small pile at her feet. Demon could see a long dress, a flowery garland and some silver jewellery.

"Put them on," she commanded, just as a chorus of despairing whinnies of pain drifted out from the mist.

"Oh no," Demon said. "Is that . . .?"

Artemis nodded, looking as worried as he'd ever seen a goddess.

"Yes. The unicorns. Hurry."

Since Demon would do pretty much anything in the world to save a sick beast, he put on his new clothes over his tunic without complaint. It felt a bit strange to be wearing a girl's dress, but when he thought about it, he supposed it wasn't all that different to wearing the Pyro-Protection suit. And if looking like a girl would help him save the unicorns, he didn't mind at all. While he was dressing himself, somehow Artemis magicked his hair long, and helped him bind it up with the flowery garland and some ribbons. Last of all, she handed him a small flask of golden liquid, which smelt strongly of lily-of-the-valley.

"Rub this all over you. It'll mask the boy scent. And remember – while you're with the unicorns, you will be Pandemonia, not Pandemonius." She turned to the hounds. "You lot had better remember it too!"

Out of the corner of his eye, Demon saw doggy grins all around him, but he didn't care. After all, Thrud had thought his tunic was odd when he first arrived in Asgard. Being a girl wasn't so hard really, he thought, right up until he tripped over the hem of his long dress and fell flat on his face. Grimacing, he picked himself up, avoiding Artemis's gaze.

"Let's go," he said. "I don't want to keep those poor beasts waiting any longer."

He walked off towards the lavender mist, not waiting for the goddess, hearing the pathetic whinnies grow louder and louder as he got closer. Demon picked up the skirts of his dress with one hand and began to run, praying his disguise would hold.

"Wait!" Artemis cried out. "You can't go . . ."

As his foot touched the lavender mist, there was a noise like a thousand silver bells, all ringing at once. Immediately, Demon was thrown backwards, a huge jet of rainbow light slamming into his chest. Flying through the air, he had just time to take one panicked breath before he thudded into the ground at the goddess's feet, scattering the hounds, who fled, howling, with their tails between their legs.

"As I was about to tell you," the goddess said crossly, "you can't enter the mist without me." She reached down and hauled him to his feet.

"Come," Artemis commanded him. "And don't let go of my hand."

8

Unicorn Emergency

This time, as Demon stepped into it, the
pale purple fog curled round him like
a cat, winding long tendrils about his
body, as if it was learning who and what
he was. He clung tightly to Artemis's
hand, which was cool and dry, with
smooth calluses where she had gripped
her bow.

Suddenly they burst through the
misty barrier and out to the other side,
followed closely by the hounds.

The unicorn lands were bathed in the

faint silver light of the crescent moon, but Demon had no time to look around.

In front of himself and the goddess stood a whole line of unicorn stallions, horns lowered, ready to protect the herd. Their ribs stuck out, and they were pitifully thin. Behind them, the pathetic whinnying of the mares and foals rose and fell like waves on the sea. Demon's heart squeezed tight with pity.

"Peace," Artemis said. "I bring you a healer."

The biggest stallion trotted forwards on shaking legs. Demon could see dark sweat on his silver-white coat.

"But the mist, beloved Goddess," he

neighed. "The bells in the mist warned of an intruder!"

"There is no intruder, Moonshadow," Artemis assured him. "Only my maiden, Pandemonia and I." She stepped forward and put a hand on his mane. "Let us through. We are here to help you."

Moonshadow shook his head.

"There is no help you can give. The time of the prophecy is at hand. Only the stars can save us now."

Demon frowned as the goddess tutted impatiently.

"What prophecy?" he asked, making his voice a little higher than normal, since he was supposed to be a girl.

The stallion's eyes fell on him. They were the shining blue of a clear summer sky.

"In the time of our foremothers, young maiden," he neighed, "there was a mare called Swifthoof. One day, she was seized by the gift of foretelling. This is what she said: In the time of the crescent shall come death out of the darkness below. The herd shall know sweetness before pain, and a long sleep with no waking. There is no help unless from the sky stars."

Moonshadow snorted softly.

"None of us knew what it meant. But it has been passed down through the generations, and now it is coming true."

"Well, whatever you believe, Moonshadow, it will do no harm to have Pandemonia look at all of you," said Artemis.

The stallion bowed his head.

"Very well, beloved Goddess," he whinnied.

As Demon put his medicine sack down, the line of stallions parted, and he walked forward between their ranks. Behind them, everywhere he could see, there were unicorn bodies littering the ground. Pathetically thin silver-white bodies, with one long white horn the exact same colour as the moonlight in the middle of their foreheads, and smaller, even thinner smoke-grey bodies with stubby horns and manes that stuck up from their tiny curved necks like messy mown grass stalks. Amidst the smell of flowers, there was a strong scent of wrongness and rot. The whinnies and groans of pain and despair all around him were heartbreaking.

"Oh no!" Demon whispered. "I think they're all dying."

The goddess stepped in front of Demon, took him by the shoulders and shook him till his teeth rattled.

"They cannot be allowed to die," she whispered fiercely, her voice frantic. "These are the last wild unicorns left on Earth, and if you cannot save them, then goodness and innocence will gradually slip away from the world.

Earth needs unicorn magic, or it will turn into a place of war and hatred."

Artemis let him go and sank to her knees, weeping, and her tears were like silver rain. Where they fell on the ground, small, frail blossoms appeared, their transparent heads drooping as if with grief.

Demon had never seen a goddess cry before, and he didn't quite know what to do. Clumsily, he bent down and patted Artemis's shoulder.

"I'll do my very best," he whispered. "I don't want them to die either." Then, picking up his medicine sack again, he approached the nearest unicorn mare, praying that his disguise would hold.

As he came near, she struggled to her feet, nickering pitifully.

"Shhh!" he said, soothingly as she trotted towards him on faltering hooves. "Shhh! I'm . . . er . . . Pandemonia. I'm here to help."

At first, as she lowered her horn, Demon thought the unicorn was going to gore him. He tensed, ready to run. But she just rested it on his shoulder and leaned her beautiful head into his chest. At least his girl disguise seemed to be holding.

"My baby," she whickered. "Save her!"

Close by, where she had been lying, Demon saw a small body. It was a unicorn foal, and it was so thin that its tiny grey body looked like it was turning to mist. As soon as he touched it, it began to thrash distressingly.

"Hush, little one, hush!" he said, though his own throat was now thick with tears. "I'm not going to hurt you."

The effort seemed to have taken the last strength from the foal, and it went limp under his hand. He could feel the rapid thump-thump hammering of its tiny heart in its chest, but that was the only sign of life.

Not for the first time in his life, Demon wished Chiron was with him. His old centaur teacher was the wisest and most knowledgeable healer there had ever been, and Demon longed for his advice. Being half a horse himself, surely he would have some idea of how to cure unicorns? But Chiron was miles away on Mount Pelion and there was no time to fetch him. Demon would have to manage on his own.

Dropping to his knees, Demon began to examine the foal. But apart from its extreme thinness, he could see nothing wrong with it on the outside.

Suddenly, all around him unicorns began to scream and thrash, including the stallions who had challenged them. It was a terrible sound, and it made Demon want to throw up with fear and panic. What was wrong with these poor beasts? And how was he ever to find a cure?

"Do something!" Artemis shouted, and

the horror in her voice made the leaves shiver. "Or I swear you will not live to see another dawn!" The hounds around her began to howl.

Demon did the only thing he could. He pulled his dad's magic pipes out of the front of his tunic and blew them.

The screaming was cut off as if with a sharp sword. Every unicorn lay still as death. Every hound lay silent on the ground. Only Demon and Artemis were left conscious.

The goddess looked at her sleeping hounds, and her eyes were like silver flames as she turned to glare at Demon. Before she could get out a word, Demon waved the pipes at her.

"I'm s-sorry, Your Celestial Shininess," he said quickly. "It was the only way. I'll wake them up again, I promise."

The goddess's eyes narrowed. "Do what you have to, Stablemaster. But do it quickly. I do not think there is much time left."

9

Red for Danger

Demon set to work at once. Many of
his patients, like the foal, had gone
misty and faint. Using all the skills
Chiron had taught him, Demon examined
each unicorn from horn to tail as best
he could in the dim light. His flowery
garland kept slipping into his eyes,
annoying him, but he didn't dare tear it
off and stamp on it as he wanted to. It
was too risky to take off any part of
his girl disguise.

Demon could still see nothing
outwardly wrong with any of the

unicorns, and he began to despair of finding anything. He rubbed at his nose absentmindedly. Then he stopped. Yes, the sweet, rotting smell he had noticed before was growing much stronger. Where was it coming from? Kneeling down beside a mare and foal, he closed his eyes and took a long breath.

"Phew!" he gasped and nearly choked. Bending down, he sniffed at the mare's mouth. Yes, that was where it was coming from!

And then, in a stray beam of moonlight, he saw a trace of red on her silver-white face. Peering closer, and lifting the mare's lip to see inside, he noticed more red smears around her teeth. The smell of sweet rot was overpowering now.

Surely this must be it, he thought, holding his nose.

Just in case, he checked the next unicorn, and the next.

There was only one thing they all had in common. Every single unicorn had red smears on its teeth. Scraping some off with a wooden spatula, Demon examined it in the faint moonlight. It definitely wasn't blood. So what was it then?

"What do unicorns eat?" he muttered to himself. The unicorn in the stables ate sun hay and ambrosia cake, like all the beasts on Olympus, but what about these wild ones?

Artemis raised her head from where she was sitting among her unconscious hounds, stroking their long ears.

"Unicorns get all their nourishment from moonlight and starlight. I don't know what Chiron has been teaching you. Everyone knows that," she said tartly.

"Well, I didn't," Demon replied, peering once again at the red smears. "Boy here, remember? I don't exactly have the most experience with unicorns." Then he suddenly remembered who he was talking to.

"I-I'm sorry, Your Celestial Shininess," he stammered. "I didn't mean . . ."

"Never mind," said the goddess, her voice impatient. "Get on with it. And don't say you're a you-know-what.

They might hear in their sleep."

There was only one thing for it.
Demon pulled the magic medicine box
out of his tunic and tapped it gently.

"Wake up, box," he said. "I need you."

Please! he thought. Please work!

After a long pause, during which
Demon tried not to grit his teeth with
impatience, the box finally flashed blue.

"Exiting emergency travel mode,"
it said, making a loud beeping sound.
Demon hurriedly set it on the ground as
it began to grow. Soon it was its normal
size again.

"State nature of ailment," it said.

"Tell me what these red smears are on the unicorn's teeth," Demon said.

Immediately the box's silver lid flipped open, and out whipped a thin bright blue tube with one large sucker on the end. It hovered over the nearest unicorn's mouth, making a slurping noise as it sucked up all the red. Then the tube disappeared back into the box.

"Initiating analysis mode," said the box. A circle of rainbow colours began to whirl on its lid.

"What is that thing?" Artemis asked.

"It's one of Hephaestus's inventions," Demon said. "I don't use it as much as I used to, but it is useful for finding stuff out quickly. It's pretty rude sometimes, but it does come up with answers."

Artemis let out a small huff of laughter, which she quickly stifled.

"That sounds like my brother Hephaestus, all right," she said. "Rude but does come up with answers. How long will it take?"

Demon shook his head.

"I don't kn—" he started to say, but as he was speaking, the rainbow circle stopped, and blue sparks shot out of the box.

"Analysis complete," it said. "Substance is pomegranate."

"Pomegranate?" Demon asked,

bewildered, looking around at the landscape. "But there's no . . ."

"Substance originates from the Underworld," the box interrupted. "Specifically from the palace gardens. No known antidote. Patient will fade away and die shortly. Thank you for your enquiry."

Then it began to beep again – a different, higher beep.

"Battery power drained. Initiating shutdown mode. Solar recharge initiating." With a whirr, its lights went out, and the box was silent. Demon tried not to kick it. He knew it would do no good. But now he really was on his own. It was not a comforting feeling.

"Hades!" Artemis snarled suddenly, leaping to her feet. "Persephone!"

Demon whirled round. "Where?" he gasped. Hades was the god of death, and Persephone was his wife. Was she here? Even worse, was he here?

Demon didn't get on with Hades at all well. He had nearly been eaten by Hades' ghost dragons once. But as his eyes flicked everywhere and fear swept over him in a great wave, he saw nobody. He let out a great sigh of relief. And then he remembered.

"Wait," he said slowly. "Hades tricked Persephone with pomegranate seeds, didn't he? And both of them tried to trap me down in the Underworld too, with pomegranate seed pasties. But . . ."

but what have pomegranates got to do with the unicorns?"

"It's the prophecy, stupid bo— I mean, GIRL!" Artemis shouted. "Think about it. In the time of the crescent shall come death out of the darkness below. That means the Underworld. And the sweetness before pain must mean the pomegranate. Hades or Persephone are the only ones who could have done this, and I'm going to make them pay!"

Whipping several arrows out of her quiver, the goddess fired them in quick succession at the earth, where they stuck for a moment, silver feathers trembling, and then disappeared downwards with a muffled whoosh.

"Will those really kill them?" Demon

asked. His personal experience of the god of death made him pretty sure that a hundred arrows wouldn't even dent him, let alone just a few. He wasn't sure how tough Persephone was, though.

"Of course not," said Artemis. "It just made me feel better. They'll give them a good sting, though."

Demon was puzzled. It still didn't make any sense.

"But why would Hades go after the unicorns?" he asked. "He's got those hell-dragons to pull his chariot, and he must have enough ghosts around to satisfy him. And I know Persephone only cares about her gardens. Orpheus told me so."

"I don't know," Artemis said, her voice grim. "Believe me, though, I will find out. But first, you need to find a cure. That stupid box of yours has to be wrong. There MUST be a way to make my unicorns better."

"The pomegranate is obviously poisoning them," Demon said slowly. "But how? It's only a fruit, really, unless you're down in the Underworld."

Artemis looked at him.

"I really DON'T know what Chiron has been teaching you," she said. "Isn't it obvious?"

It was quite hard to think with a goddess glaring at him as if she wanted to turn him into a beetle. She obviously wasnt going to tell him what she knew. Demon began to pace, his brain whirling. Then he smacked himself in the forehead. It was obvious.

"The unicorns are creatures of light," he cried triumphantly. "And those pomegranates come from the Underworld where it's all dark. No wonder it's poisoning them."

Then he frowned.

"It's a pity I don't have any of Hestia's fire left," Demon said. "That might have helped. But I used it all on Goldbristle the Boar when I was in Asgard."

Artemis raised one thin eyebrow.

"Are you allowed to use that?" she

asked. "Zeus gets very cross if the fire is taken off Olympus. Why, poor Prometheus . . ."

"I know all about Prometheus having his liver torn out by the Caucausian Eagle every day," Demon interrupted her hastily. "But it's all right. Hestia's fine with me having her fire. I didn't steal it or anything."

He carefully didn't say that in fact Zeus had no idea about his arrangement with the goddess of the kitchens.

Just then all the unicorns began to thrash and moan again, and one of the hounds let out a whimper.

"Oh no!" Demon said. "They're waking up."

10

The Missing Ingredient

Demon reached frantically for his pipes,
putting them to his lips and blowing
a short, sharp blast. Immediately
all the beasts slumped back into
unconsciousness.

What else did he have that he could
use? Since the box was now useless,
Demon began to rummage in his
medicine sack.

"Sunflowers," he said to Artemis.
"They're good light medicine. And
I think I have some essence of

moonflower too, Maybe a combination
of those will do it."

Quickly, Demon tipped some dried
sunflower petals into his mortar and
ground them up with a little oil, then
added a few drops of the moonflower
essence. When he had finished, he had
a sticky gloop that glowed a pale gold.

Gently levering one of the mistiest
mare's teeth open with a nearby stick,
he tipped a few drops of the mixture
in.

Nothing happened, so he dropped
in one more.

Still nothing.

"It's not doing anything," he said,

feeling despair steal over him like a cloud.

"Then think of something else that will," Artemis growled at him. "And be quick about it. Because the foals are getting worse."

It was true. Some of the foals were now nothing more than a misty outline on the ground.

Demon wanted to howl with frustration. There must be something. What was he missing? Then his eyes fell on the sickle moon, now halfway across the sky. Maybe that was why the unicorns were so thin. Maybe they'd been fighting the pomegranate poison off so hard that they were starving!

What had the prophecy said? There is no help unless from the sky stars. And what was the moon if not a kind of sky star?

"The moon, Your Silvery Serenity," he said, excitement rising in his voice. "Can you influence the moon?"

Artemis looked at him.

"Of course," she said. "I am a moon goddess, after all. But why?"

Demon spluttered out his theory.

"I need you to make it full," he finished. "I think a proper dose of moonlight will cure them."

"Very well," said Artemis. "But Selene

will not be pleased if I meddle for too long. She's in charge of moon matters."

With that, she pulled out an arrow, bigger and brighter than the rest, and attached it to a ball of silver twine she drew out of thin air. Then she fitted the arrow to the bow, pulled it back and fired.

Immediately the tethered arrow sped high into the sky, higher and higher until it was no more than a silver spark in the darkness. Then Demon saw the moon tremble as it hit.

Slowly, hand over hand, Artemis drew in the twine. And as she did so, the moon moved. Closer and closer it came to earth, and as it did so, the shadows dropped away from it, revealing more and more of its silvery orb, until it was round and full and fat. Gradually, the night landscape lit up, until the unicorns were bathed in a light nearly as bright as day.

One-handed, Artemis tied another arrow to the twine and fired it into a large rock nearby.

'There!" she said. "That should hold it till moonset."

But Demon wasn't looking at her or the moon. He was looking at the unicorns. Already the misty foals were firming up, and the adult unicorns were growing a little fatter. The moonlight was feeding them.

"Look, Your Moonlight Magnificence!" he said. "It's working!"

"Then wake them up," Artemis said.

Demon blew the wake up call, and all around him unicorns began to scramble to their feet. But almost immediately, Demon knew that something was still wrong.

A small breeze wafted a delicious scent towards him, and as one, the herd bunched together, totally silent, their horns all facing one way. With a neighing scream, they tottered forward on unsteady legs towards a grove of trees a little way off.

"Sweet, sweet, sweet!" they neighed, as they crashed in among the trees. "Must have more sweet!"

In the moonlight, Demon spotted

golden balls hanging from the black-leafed branches. The unicorns shouldered each other out of the way in their eagerness to get at them.

"Oh no!" he yelled, beginning to run. "They're eating pomegranates again!"

Pulling his pipes out, Demon blew again desperately. As if they were cut strings, the unicorns collapsed together in a heap, their look of health fading as quickly as it had appeared. But when Demon reached the grove, the sweet smell became overpowering, so delicious that it made his mouth water. He found his hand reaching out towards one of the deadly fruits.

"STOP!" shouted Artemis, grabbing Demon round the waist and lifting him up. Demon struggled as she dragged him back towards the hounds. As soon as he was away from the smell, she flung him down.

"STAY!" she hissed, and her voice was deadlier than a nest of angry vipers.

Striding back towards the grove again, the goddess reached up to the moon, drawing down several of its yellow-white beams into her hands. Shaping them into balls as she went, she began flinging them at the pomegranate trees.

As each ball hit a tree, it exploded with a flash of brightness. Soon there were no more trees left, only a deep pit in the ground. But the goddess didn't stop. Pulling down more and more moonbeams, she filled the pit, until it was a lake brimming with light.

Stalking back to where Demon lay, Artemis reached down and picked him up by the front of his dress. Her eyes were like silver fire, and he quaked as she looked at him.

"You have failed me, Stablemaster," the goddess said in a voice so quiet and menacing that he went still and limp with fear. Her grip tightened. "I may have destroyed Persephone's trees, but my unicorns still look very sick. You have not kept your promise. I think I shall give you to my hounds after all. Your father will forgive me. Eventually."

"P-p-please," Demon gasped. "Give me one more chance, Your B-Bright Beautifulness. I will try again. I WILL cure them properly this time."

Artemis dropped him disdainfully.

"You have until moonset, Stablemaster. I will be back from the Underworld by then. I go to punish my uncle and his wife. If you fail, not only will I give you to my hounds, but I will set my bears on you too."

With that, the goddess dived into the moonlight lake she had created, and disappeared.

Demon stood there for a moment, breathing hard. His heart was crashing around in his chest like one of the fiery bulls on a rampage. He ran his hands through his too-long hair, and tried not to panic.

"What shall I use? What shall I use? Think, Demon!" he muttered to himself. Sunflowers and essence of moonflower hadn't worked, though the moonlight had made a difference. But maybe if he added something, something that would turn them back to eating moonshine and starlight and encourage them to forget the sweet pomegranate seeds. What else had he got?

Tipping everything out of his medicine sack he sorted through it frantically.

"Not that, not that, not that," he said, casting rue and willowbark and peppermint aside. Then something golden caught his eye. It was a ball of fleece from the Golden Ram. That shines pretty bright, he thought, setting it aside.

He was just getting up to fetch some of the silvery flowers which had grown out of Artemis's tears, when he felt someone brush against his arm, and tug on his dress. Demon turned round. This was getting ridiculous.

"Who ARE you?" he demanded. But there was no reply.

Instead, a small wide-necked bottle half full of dark dust rolled across the ground towards him, tinkling slightly. The sight of it tickled his memory. It was the stardust he had gathered on the way to send Typhon back to sleep.

"That's it!" he shouted, his voice echoing back at him in the eerie silence. "That's the missing sky star ingredient!"

As if his brain had suddenly added everything up, Demon now knew exactly what to do. Working fast, he plucked some of Artemis's silver tearflowers and put them in his mortar. After that, he shook in some more sunflower petals and moonflower essence, and flipped in the ball of golden wool. Then he ran over to the moonlight lake and dipped out a measure of what seemed to be liquid light. A little of it slopped onto his fingers, where it fizzed slightly, with a feeling like hot ice.

Carefully, he mixed and pounded everything together, then, last of all, he tipped in half of the stardust. As soon as it hit the surface of the new potion, it began to sparkle. The whole mixture began to bubble, emitting a light so bright that Demon had to squint against it as he carried the mortar carefully over to the heap of fallen unicorns.

One by one, very carefully, he fed a drop into each unicorn's mouth. When the potion touched the red stains of the pomegranate, they immediately disappeared with a sizzle. By the time he was finished, there was only a scrape of potion in the bottom of the mortar, and all the unicorns looked sleek and healthy again.

Demon closed his eyes, and pulled his pipes out for the fifth time that night. Putting them to his lips and crossing every one of his toes, since his fingers weren't available, he blew a series of trills, hoping against hope for a miracle.

11

Feast in the Forest

Almost immediately, Demon was surrounded by snuffling noses, waggy tails and happy howls. The hounds had woken and come galumphing towards him on their huge paws.

"We're awake, we're awake, we're awake!" they woofed.

As Demon blew one last trill, Moonshadow lifted his head. Then all the unicorns were surrounding him as well, the foals nuzzling him with their soft noses, their little whisks of tails flicking from side to side.

"Are you well?" Demon asked anxiously, remembering to pitch his voice a little higher again. He just hoped the flower scent Artemis had made him put on was holding. He still had to be Pandemonia.

"Never be-he-hetter!" Moonshadow whinnied. "And all thanks to you and our Beloved Goddess!"

"What exactly happened to you?" Demon asked. "Why did you eat the pomegranates?"

The mare who had asked him to save her foal pushed through the crowd of horned heads.

"As far as I remember it," she whinnied, "there was a bang from over there, just before moonrise. It was just as the prophecy said. A big clot of darkness erupted out of the earth, and then we smelled it. The sweetness. It was so delicious that we couldn't resist, but once we'd eaten it the pain came, and we started to die. I don't really remember anything much after that." She shuddered. "I never want to see or smell that horrid stuff ever again."

As she finished, Demon noticed a large group of unicorns trot over to where the things from his medicine sack lay strewn across the ground.

"Don't eat any of that," he cried, but he needn't have worried. The unicorns weren't interested in his sack. Instead they were neighing in welcome. Demon peered over to see who had come, but there appeared to be nobody there.

He suddenly remembered the tug on his dress, and the continual feeling of being watched, which he'd had ever since he returned to Olympus.

"Who is that they're greeting?" he asked the mare casually, holding his breath in anticipation.

"Oh, that's our friend Electra," she whinnied. "I'm surprised you can see her. She's usually invisible."

Suddenly Demon remembered what Alcyone had said to him in the sun boat.

Electra's invisible . . . she's rather
shy. I think she might like you!

The seventh of the Pleiades must
have followed him!

"Oh, Electra!" Demon called. "Why
don't you come and say hello? I want to
say thank you!"

A tiny soft giggle reached him, and
then, in the middle of the unicorns, a
light began to shine. It revealed a small,
plump girl, wearing a crown of living
stars. As Demon stared, she floated
over to him, her feet seeming not to
touch the ground.

"You do look funny in a dress," she
whispered in his ear. Demon blushed.

"I had to," he whispered back. "It's a disguise."

She smiled and reached out to tug his ribbons and adjust his garland, which had slipped over one eye again, just as the full moon sank behind the trees, pulling Artemis's arrow out of the rock with a small pop.

Almost immediately, Artemis rose from the moonlight lake, trailing moonbeams from her robe. Her face lit up as she saw the unicorns, many of them drinking from their new lake.

"Well, Pandemonia," she said. "I see my hounds and bears will have to go hungry."

"He did very well," said Electra,

floating over and curtsying to the goddess. "I only had to give him the tiniest of hints."

Demon couldn't contain his curiosity any longer.

"What happened in the Underworld, if you don't mind me asking, Your Celestial Shininess?"

Artemis laughed.

"It all turned out to be a big mistake," she said. "Hades and Persephone were having one of their eternal arguments in the garden, and Persephone pulled up all the pomegranate trees in a temper and flung them at him. Hades threw a darkness bolt at them, and it was so strong that it carried them all the way up here. Of course, because Persephone had touched them, they grew where they fell. They were both very apologetic when they'd finished picking my arrows out of themselves. They both know how important my unicorns are."

Demon tried to imagine arguing with the god of death and winning. He failed miserably.

"He . . . er . . . he's not coming up here, is he?" he asked nervously.

"No," said Artemis. "But now I come to think of it, he did send you a message."

Demon gulped.

"W-what was it?"

"He said to tell you that the position of keeper to the ghost dragons is still open," the goddess replied.

Demon shuddered. That was definitely not a job he wanted.

"I think I'll pass," he said quite firmly.

"A sensible decision," said Artemis. "And now, I think that we should have a feast in honour of the unicorns' recovery."

Demon's tummy rumbled loudly. He couldn't remember when he'd last eaten, and he was suddenly VERY hungry.

"What a brilliant idea, Your Amazing Archeriness," he said, grinning. For all her threats, Artemis was pretty nice for a goddess, he thought.

A short while later six beams of light fell out of the sky. Electra had summoned her sisters to the celebration. Before they sat down to the feast, the Pleiades poured handfuls of starshine into the new lake, which sparkled with a million rainbow colours in the light of dawn. All the unicorns gathered round to drink, and as they did so, their coats began to glow with a soft light. The final effects of the pomegranate disappeared as if they had never been.

"Why did you follow me?" Demon

asked Electra as he tucked into mushroom patties as light as air, and little baked chestnuts rolled in honey and crunchy brown sugar. He didn't know where Artemis had conjured the feast from, but he suspected Hestia had had something to do with it.

Electra's shining cheeks turned a little pink.

"Well," she said slowly, "I've always been the curious one of us seven. I like to learn new things – and you're so fascinating with those pipes of yours and, well . . . I liked you. I don't have many friends, other than my sisters," she said, turning even pinker.

Demon felt his own cheeks mirroring hers.

"Well, you can be my friend if you like," he said. "Only next time, perhaps you might like to let me know you're there. It's a bit hard to be friendly when I can't see you."

"Hey, Stablemaster," Alcyone called over in a teasing voice. "What are you saying to my sister to make her turn the colour of Eos's curtains, young man?"

Her words fell into a sudden deep silence.

"What?" she asked, sounding puzzled, as the unicorns all crowded round, sniffing at Demon suspiciously. "What have I said?"

"Did I hear you ri-hi-hight?" Moonshadow neighed, rearing up.

"Is Pandemonia a BOY?"

Artemis held up her hands as his hooves thudded to the ground.

"Yes," she said. "He is."

"You lied to us, Beloved Goddess," he trumpeted. "You broke our rules! No boys! No men!"

"Yes, I did," said Artemis, rising to face him. "And it was for your own good. Has Pandemonius done you any harm? No. He has healed you. So what if I disguised him a little?"

Moonshadow's head fell, and he let out a breathy sigh that smelled of moon and stars. The other unicorns watched him.

"Very well," he whinnied. "It is true, he has done us a great service. So from now on, while he is in our lands, he shall be an honorary girl, and he shall have the protection and goodwill of all unicorns."

He stamped one hoof.

"Come here, Pandemonius." Demon approached the unicorn warily, keeping his eyes on Moonshadow's very long, pointy horn. The stallion knelt down in front of him. "Take my horn, and break off the tip, then take it to our Beloved Goddess."

Demon flinched. "Won't that hurt you?" he asked.

Moonshadow let out a snort of horsey

laughter, and Artemis rolled her eyes at his ignorance.

"Not at all," he said. "It will grow back in a trice."

So Demon set his hands on the horn, which felt warm and smooth, like silk over smooth, hot rock and snapped off the very end. Moonshadow was right. It grew back at once. He took it over to Artemis and put it in her hands.

Taking a piece of the silver twine she had used to pull down the moon, the goddess twisted both ends round the broken bit of the horn, winding it round and round so that it hung from a long string. Then she put it over Demon's head, tucking it down into the front of his tunic underneath his dress.

"There," Artemis said. "May the favour of the unicorns be with you always."

"Thank you, Your Celestial Shininess," Demon said, bowing. "And thank you, Moonshadow."

He stepped backwards, tripped over the hem of his dress and promptly fell over.

"Please can I take this off?" Demon asked plaintively. "I'm fed up with tripping over. And can I lose the long hair? It's really hot on my neck!"

Artemis and all the Pleiades laughed.

"Certainly not," the goddess said. "Moonshadow has already had enough shocks for one day . . . Pandemonia."

Demon sighed.

He supposed, all things considered, a dress and long hair weren't really that bad. And the garland did smell awfully nice.

He reached for another mushroom patty, and turned to Electra.

"So, my invisible friend," he said. "About this being-a-girl stuff. Do you have any handy hints?"

GLOSSARY
Pronunciation Guide

The Greek Gods:

Ares *(AIR-eez)*: God of war. Loves any excuse to pick a fight.

Artemis *(AR-te-miss)*: Goddess of the hunt. Can't decide if she wants to protect animals or kill them.

Chiron *(KY-ron)*: God of the centaurs. Known for his wisdom and healing abilities.

Demeter *(duh-MEE-ter)*: Goddess of plants and the harvest. The original green thumb.

Dionysus *(DY-uh-NY-suss)*: God of wine. Turns even sensible gods into silly goons.

Hades *(HAY-deez)*: Zeus's brother and the gloomy, fearsome ruler of the Underworld.

Helios (*HEE-lee-us*): The bright, shiny, and blinding Titan god of the sun.

Hephaestus (*hih-FESS-tuss*): God of blacksmithing, metalworking, fire, volcanoes, and most things awesome.

Hera (*HEER-a*): Zeus's scary wife. Drives a chariot pulled by screechy peacocks.

Hestia (*HESS-tee-ah*): Goddess of the hearth and home. Bakes the most heavenly treats.

Pan (*PAN*): God of shepherds and flocks. Frequently found wandering grassy hillsides, playing his pipes.

Persephone (*per-SEF-oh-nee*): Goddess of Spring, stolen away by Hades to be his wife. Made bad mistake of eating pomegranate seeds in the Underworld.

Zeus (*ZOOSS*): King of the gods. Fond of smiting people with lightning bolts.

The Norse Gods:

Frey *(FRAY)*: Shiny, happy god of peace, growth, and sunshine. Twin brother of Freya.

Freya *(FRAY-uh)*: Goddess of love and beauty. Twin sister of Frey.

Heimdall *(HAME-doll)*: Guardian and herald of Asgard. Has a really loud horn.

Idunn *(ih-DOON)*: Goddess who grows golden apples that make you live forever.

Loki *(LOW-kee)*: The sneaky, shape-shifting trickster god of Asgard.

Odin *(OH-dinn)*: The All-Father and ruler of Asgard.

Thor *(THOR)*: Mighty god of thunder who has a giant hammer called Mjölnir *(MYAWL-neer)*.

Thrud *(THROOD)*: Thor's daughter. Well on her way to becoming a Valkyrie.

Other Mythical Beings:

Amaltheia *(ah-mul-THEE-uh)*: An actual goat who raised Zeus as if he were her own kid.

Cherubs *(CHAIR-ubs)*: Small flying babies. Mostly cute.

Dryads *(DRY-ads)*: Tree nymphs. Can literally sing trees to life.

Heracles *(HAIR-a-kleez)*: The half-god "hero" who just loooves killing magical beasts.

Morpheus *(MOR-fee-us)*: The spirit of dreams. Brings wonderful (or terrible) visions to the sleeping.

Nymphs (*NIMFS*): Giggly, girly, dancing nature spirits.

Orpheus (*OR-fee-us*): A musician, a poet, and a real charmer.

Valkyries (*VAL-kuh-reez*): The shield-maidens who bring fallen heroes to Valhalla.

Places:

Asgard (*ASS-gard*): The chilly Northern home of the Norse gods.

Mount Pelion (*PEEL-ee-un*): A mountain on the Aegean Sea where Chiron the centaur lives.

Svartalfheim (*SVART-alf-hame*): Creepy underground home of the dark elves.

Valhalla (*vall-HALL-uh*): Official party hall for the heroes and Valkyries.

Yggdrasil (*IGG-druh-sill*): A giant ash tree that keeps the whole world together.

Beasts:

Centaur *(SEN-tor):* Half man, half horse, and lucky enough to get the best parts of both.

Colchian Dragon *(KOL-kee-un):* Ares's guard dragon turned Heffy's helper. Has magical teeth and *supposedly* never sleeps. Rather gassy.

Cretan Bull *(KREE-tun):* A furious, fire-breathing bull. Don't stand too close.

Fafnir *(FAVE-neer):* A fearsome cursed dragon who guards a stash of gems and gold.

Fenrir *(FEN-reer):* Mad wolf who has it in for Odin.

Griffin *(GRIH-fin):* Couldn't decide if it was better to be a lion or an eagle, so decided to be both.

Gullinbursti *(GOO-lin-burst-ee):* Also known as Goldbristle, he's a glowing golden boar and friend of Frey.

Hydra *(HY-druh)*: Nine-headed water serpent. Hera somehow finds this lovable.

Pegasus *(PEG-uh-sus)*: The mightiest winged horse of all.

Phoenix *(FEE-nix)*: Wondrous bird with a burning desire to be reborn every hundred years.

Ratatosk *(RAH-tah-tosk)*: A red messenger squirrel who runs around in the tree Yggdrasil.

Unicorn *(YOO-ni-corn)*: Magical moonlight horses with a single horn. Not fond of men or boys.

Have you read them all?

Out now, in all places good books are sold.